DATE DUE

ALIENS IN WOODFORD

ALIENS IN WOODFORD

MARY LABATT

KIDS CAN PRESS

Kids Can Press acknowledges the financial support of the Ontario Arts Council, the Canada Council for the Arts and the Department of Cultural Heritage.

Published in Canada by
Kids Can Press Ltd.
29 Birch Avenue
Toronto, ON M4V 1E2

Published in the U.S. by
Kids Can Press Ltd.
4500 Witmer Estates
Niagara Falls, NY 14305-1386

Edited by Charis Wahl
Designed by Marie Bartholomew
Typeset by Karen Birkemoe
Printed and bound in Canada

CM 00 0 9 8 7 6 5 4 3 2 1
CM PA 00 0 9 8 7 6 5 4 3 2 1

Canadian Cataloguing in Publication Data

Labatt, Mary, date
    Aliens in Woodford

(Sam, dog detective)
ISBN 1-55074-611-1 (bound)   ISBN 1-55074-607-3 (pbk.)

I. Title. II. Series: Labatt, Mary, date. Sam, dog detective.

PS8573.A135A83 2000   jC813'.54   C99-933008-X
PZ7.L1155 Al 2000

Kids Can Press is a Nelvana company

For my son, Anthony,
Who loves an adventure story,
With my love

1. Strange Lights at Night

EXCITEMENT AT LAST!

Hey! I see the light again!

It was the middle of the night and Sam was looking out her favorite upstairs window. From there, she could see past the houses into the countryside around Woodford. Lately she had noticed something different.

In a field at the edge of town, small round lights bobbed up and down. Down and up. Up and down. Like a strange, silent dance.

Wow, this is weird! thought Sam happily. *This is the third night I've seen lights in that field!*

Strange things always made Sam hungry, so she ambled downstairs to find something to eat. The house was quiet except for loud rumbling snores coming from Joan and Bob's bedroom.

In the living room, moonbeams streamed through the window. Sam nosed under the sofa cushions until she found a piece of candy.

Sitting in bright silvery moonlight, Sam crunched noisily. *I wonder what those lights are. Hmm ... They start when everybody's asleep ... They don't make a sound ... They're always in that field.*

When Sam couldn't find any more candy, she climbed the stairs and looked out the hall window again. The lights were still there. Down and up. Up and down.

Very strange.

Later, Sam crawled up on the spare bed. She turned around and settled herself comfortably. Nestling her chin on her paws, she let her mind wander. Mysterious lights, goblins and witches whirled in her thoughts. Those were the things Sam loved.

Sam snuggled into the pillows and sighed happily. *About time we had some excitement in Woodford. It's been so boring lately, I'm half dead.*

Boredom is bad.

Mornings were busy at Sam's house. Joan always offered her a bowl of disgusting dog food. Then Bob took her outside on a leash, which made Sam feel ridiculous. She didn't need a leash. When they got back, there was always a flurry of briefcases and quick bites of toast. Then Joan and Bob rushed out to work, the door slammed and Sam was alone.

I shouldn't be stuck in this stupid house. I'm a famous detective. I should be out solving my new case.

She wandered over to the kitchen window and saw Jennie leave for school. Ten-year-old Jennie Levinsky was Sam's next-door neighbor. Joan and Bob had hired Jennie to take Sam for walks after school. Now she was Sam's best friend.

Sam hopped up on the living room sofa to sulk until school was over. The hours dragged past.

At last, the key turned in the front door!

Sam pounced on Jennie and covered her face with huge slurps. *You're never going to believe what I've found!* She squinted into Jennie's soft brown eyes.

Jennie could hear what Sam thought. She grinned and threw her schoolbag on the floor. "What have you found, Sam?"

Sam chortled happily. *Excitement. That's what.*

"You're such a weird dog!" Jennie giggled. "Nobody needs excitement all the time."

The hair over Sam's eyes moved up and down. *I am not weird. Boredom is bad for a person. People can die of boredom.*

"The only person who thinks they'll die of boredom is you." Jennie patted Sam's big head. "And you're not a person. You're a dog."

Well, I'm no ordinary dog. Like a mountain of fur, Sam flopped on the floor. *I'm a famous detective, and I have nothing to detect.*

Jennie giggled again. Sam's thoughts rang in Jennie's head in a hollow, echoing way. It was just like talking, only it wasn't out loud.

No one else could hear Sam. Not even

Jennie's best friend, Beth Morrison. Sam had told Jennie that she had a special gift. *I can always tell when someone's got it. Most dogs are too stupid to notice.*

Sam nudged Jennie with her fat black nose. *Well? Do you want to know what's so exciting, or don't you?*

"Of course I do." Jennie smiled. "What's so exciting?"

Lights.

"Lights?"

Yup. They're in a field at the edge of town. At night. I can see them from upstairs. They bounce all over the field.

"Where do they come from?"

I don't know. But they only come when everybody's asleep. Sam thought for a moment. *Want to know something really weird?*

"What?"

Those lights must be sneaky. They don't make any noise.

Jennie looked puzzled. "If it's lawn mowers or machines or something, you'd hear motors."

There are no motors. The lights are silent.

"Maybe they're searchlights. Somebody is looking at the sky."

Sam shook her head. *They're not searchlights.*

"How do you know?"

Because the lights don't look at the sky. They just bob up and down.

Jennie chewed her lip. "That is weird."

Something exciting is happening! Sam looked hard at Jennie. *I can feel it, Jennie. This is my new case.*

Sam started humming to herself. *So ... here's the mystery.*

Why would silent lights bob around a field?

2. What Do the Lights Mean?

The lights came back that night. As Sam watched their mysterious bouncing, her head buzzed with happiness. *Wonderful!*

Sam waited all day to tell Jennie. As the hours passed, she paced and fretted and grumbled in the empty house.

When Jennie and Beth came in after school, Sam jumped all over them. *About time you got here! I have news! But first I need food.*

Jennie laughed. "We'll go to my house, Sam. I'll make you some popcorn."

Sam dashed to the front door. *Quick! I'm starving.*

Jennie's thirteen-year-old brother, Noel, met them at the front door.

"Well, if it isn't Samantha, the walking mop." Sam glared.

Noel took a huge bite of his peanut butter sandwich. "Don't feed that dog any junk food, Jennie," he warned through sandwich globs. "I'll tell Mom, and you'll be in trouble."

Who made you the boss of the world?

"I'm going to play baseball down the street." Noel walked across the lawn backward, punching his catcher's mitt. "I'm supposed to baby-sit you. But since you're not a baby, just call me if you need me."

We won't need you. Nobody needs teenagers.

Jennie and Beth went inside, made popcorn and took it up to Jennie's room. Jennie put two bowls on the floor for Sam, one filled with popcorn and the other with root beer.

Sam eyed the popcorn with distaste. *This needs some zip. Where's the ketchup?*

Sighing, Jennie went downstairs and came back with a bottle of ketchup.

Beth giggled. "Nobody puts ketchup on popcorn."

I'd like some chocolate sauce, too.

"We're out of chocolate sauce, Sam." Jennie was firm.

Sadly, Sam went back to her popcorn. *Some pickles would be nice.*

"No pickles!" Jennie watched Sam crossly. "Noel's right. You should eat dog food!"

Aaaagh! Don't even talk about dog food. Sam shuddered. *I might throw up. Joan tried to make me eat Liver Delight last night.*

Beth looked up from her computer game. "Ask Sam about the strange lights she saw, Jennie. Maybe we have a new mystery."

Beth is such a nice kid.

"I don't want a new mystery. Mysteries always mean trouble."

Personally, I love trouble.

Beth thought about the lights. "Maybe it's robbers burying their loot at night."

"Robbers?"

"Yeah." Beth's green eyes sparkled and her red hair bounced. "Robbers need a place to put money and jewels, don't they?"

Jennie chewed her lip. "Couldn't they just put stuff in a basement?"

Sam stopped eating. *Robbers would be good. I'd like to catch a gang of robbers.* She pictured herself getting a reward. Cameras flashed and people cheered. "Sam is the wonder dog!" they cried.

"It can't be robbers," decided Jennie. "The police would see them."

Sam thought about the way the lights danced up and down. *Maybe it's elves.*

"Elves?"

Beth looked interested.

Yeah. Tell her, Jennie. Elves dancing around a toadstool. Rabbits pulling their carts. Toads doing all the work in their village. You know — little people who live in the woods.

Jennie twirled her long hair thoughtfully. "Sam thinks elves might be doing magic dances around a toadstool. Stuff like that."

Beth's face grew dreamy. "I'd love to see elves."

Sam started to pace. *Or maybe it's witches. They have meetings at night holding torches. It could be witches chanting their evil chants and mixing their horrible brew.* Sam hummed happily. *Wonderful! Old hags with warts and long noses.*

Jennie rolled her eyes. "Now Sam thinks it's witches."

But Sam wasn't finished. *Hey! Maybe it's some spooky cult that chants at the moon ... You know — a ceremony where they sacrifice animals ...* Sam gulped. *I hope it's not dogs.*

Jennie snorted. "Now Sam's talking about a spooky cult that sacrifices animals."

"This is great!" Beth started to pace back and forth with Sam. "I really want to know what those lights are."

"Not me." Jennie shook her head.

Let's go take a look.

"We can't look, Sam. The lights only come when we're sleeping."

So, set your alarm and wake up.

"My parents wouldn't let me go out at night."

Beth was watching Sam and Jennie. "How can we get a close look at those lights? There's got to be a way."

"There is no way."

"Yes there is!" Beth snapped her fingers. "A sleepover! Then we could sneak out."

The kid's got brains, Jennie.

Jennie shook her head again. "I'd be grounded for the rest of my life."

Beth paced harder. "Come on, Jennie. We can sleep at my house."

Sam glared. *A nice mystery pops into my boring life and you just sit there.*

Jennie folded her arms firmly. "I don't want to wander around at night."

Sam's mind started to whir. *I've got it! The greatest plan in the world! Naturally, since it comes from me – the world's greatest detective.*

Jennie groaned.

We'll sleep in a tent. Then we can sneak over to the field whenever we want.

"Are you crazy, Sam? I told you. We're not sneaking out at night!"

Sam sniffed. *We'll see.*

3. Sam Watches Television

That night, Joan and Bob settled down on the sofa to watch a movie on television.

This better be good. Sam grunted as she stretched out on the rug. *I hate boring movies almost as much as I hate lying on the floor.*

Sam watched as a spaceship landed in the woods. Wild-looking outer-space creatures swarmed off the ship. Like spiders they scuttled along, waving their countless legs and arms. Chattering to one another, they crashed through the underbrush.

Ho hum. Who cares about a bunch of three-headed little weirdos?

At that moment, the scene changed to a

lonely farmhouse in the middle of moonlit fields. Chitter. Chitter. Gabble. Gabble. The creatures crawled over the fences and streamed toward the house.

The house was dark and silent.

Chitter, chitter, chitter. The creatures thronged around the windows and doors.

Sam sat up. *Watch out, you people in the farmhouse! Wake up!*

"Let's see if we can find something better," suggested Bob, flipping the channel.

Hey! Change that back! I want to see what happens!

But the television flipped from scene to scene. Cars zooming, people drinking coffee, elephants dancing. Then the movie appeared again.

The creatures had spider threads coming out of their long fingers and toes. Sam watched in horror. *Uh-oh. They're wrapping somebody up!*

Zap. The screen flashed to ice skating.

Quit that! Get back to the movie.

Zap. A small boy was eating cereal. Zap. Back

to the movie. The creatures lugged all the wrapped people out of the house. One of the aliens pressed something on his belt and a light flashed off and on. He pointed the light skyward.

Out of the dark sky zoomed a spaceship — round, eerie and silent. Whoosh. It landed in a field and its huge doors drew back. Light streamed from the opening.

Chitter. Chitter. Waving their arms and heads, the little creatures dragged their victims toward the spaceship. Gabble. Gabble. They thronged onto the spacecraft and disappeared into the bright light.

Without a sound, the spaceship rose and hovered over the house. Then with a swoosh it vanished into the dark sky and was gone.

Wow! Sam lay down as the television flashed to the empty farmhouse. *Those little guys are creepy.*

Zap again. A chef was cooking pasta.

Boring. Sam got up, went to the front door and scratched.

"Want to go out, Sam?" asked Joan.

Sam whined.

Joan opened the door and Sam stepped out into the night. She sat on the porch and looked up at the starry sky. Silent stars twinkled back at her.

High in the sky, a light blinked as it passed overhead. *I bet that's a spaceship.*

Sam thought about three-headed creatures with spidery fingers. She thought about the way they signaled with a light. She thought about the soundless spaceship zooming into outer space.

The dark sky beckoned to her with its mysteries. It spoke of a universe that stretched forever – of secret worlds and strange creatures no one has ever seen.

Now ... this is what I call interesting.

In Jennie's bedroom the next day, Sam told Jennie she had another idea about the lights.

Jennie was not impressed. "Forget it."

But what if the lights are creatures from outer space?

"Like Martians?"

Yeah. These outer-space guys on TV wrapped everybody up in spiderwebs.

In spite of herself, Jennie was interested. "Sam thinks those lights might be aliens. What do you think, Beth?"

Beth thought for a moment. "I'm not sure. Let's make a list of all the possibilities."

List? Sam's head whipped up. *We're talking about exciting stuff and this kid wants to start writing!*

Sam bumped Jennie's leg. *Tell your friend if she writes one word, I'll bite.*

"Look out, Beth," giggled Jennie. "If you start writing, Sam's going to bite."

Beth hooted.

Sam sniffed. *Well … I could bite. I am the toughest dog in town.*

Jennie snorted. "Sam wants us to know she's the toughest dog in Woodford."

"Okay. I promise I won't write anything."

Beth slid off the bed. "The idea of aliens is a good one. Let's go to the library and get some books about outer space."

Sam rolled her eyes. *Now there's another big waste of time.*

"But, Sam, we need to find out about aliens," Jennie objected.

I don't want to find out about them. I want to catch one! I'll be famous.

Jennie heaved a worried sigh. "Sam, nobody catches aliens."

Think of it, Jennie. I'll be on all the magazine covers.

Sam — the famous alien catcher.

4. All about Aliens

DO THEY
BOTHER DOGS?

After school the next day, the three friends went to Jennie's room. The girls read for so long that Sam was getting crabby.

Hurry up! I haven't had a snack for hours.

Jennie looked up from her book. "This stuff is really interesting."

I'm hungry.

"Look at these creatures — buggy eyes, huge heads, long fingers with suction cups on them." Jennie held up a picture. "Yuck!"

They're almost as ugly as teenagers.

"The aliens in this book are super intelligent. They can think faster than any human." Beth chewed her fingernails as she read.

Jennie turned a page. "These aliens see through walls!" She pointed to a picture of a battle. An army was spraying aliens with foam from huge guns. "In this book, they stopped them with foam. The creatures got stuck in it."

Suddenly Beth gasped. "The government knows aliens land here!" She pointed to the big print at the top of a page: 'The Truth about UFOs.' "Lots of people have seen UFOs and the government's keeping it secret!"

"What's a UFO?"

"It stands for Unidentified Flying Object. The government has secret files on all the UFOs people have seen!"

Why would they keep it secret? Sam shoved her nose into Jennie's arm. *Aliens are big news.*

"Maybe they think people will panic." Jennie peered over Beth's shoulder and gulped. "Hey! People have been kidnapped!"

"Here's a man who remembers being taken up into a spaceship." Beth's face paled. "The aliens studied him, and then they brought him back home."

Jennie flipped a few more pages. "Uh-oh. Here's a family that disappeared after a lot of UFOs were seen around their house. Nobody ever saw them again."

Sounds like the farmhouse in that movie. I wonder why the aliens want people ... Suddenly Sam sat up straight. *Maybe the aliens put people in a zoo! I bet they'd feed you disgusting food.*

Jennie shuddered. "That's a terrible thought."

Beth stopped reading. "What's terrible?"

"Sam's talking about being taken prisoner by aliens and being put in a zoo."

Beth's eyes widened. Then she went back to her book.

Jennie swallowed nervously.

Let me tell you, those spider guys on TV were really weird.

"Here's something worse than getting kidnapped!" Beth shrieked.

"Worse?" exclaimed Jennie. "How can it get worse?"

"Aliens take over people's bodies!"

"What!"

"Yeah. Then they look exactly like human beings. See! It says so right here! They use people's bodies, but inside they're really aliens."

Sam gulped. *Do they take over dogs?*

"Do they take over dogs, Beth?"

Beth shrugged. "Probably."

Sam pictured a swarm of aliens climbing down people's throats. When the people tried to speak, no words came out. All they could say was, "Chitter. Chitter. Gabble. Gabble." She shivered.

I think I'll keep my mouth shut for a while. Just in case.

5. The Old Airfield

On Saturday morning, Sam decided they should go to the field and look for clues. So Jennie, Beth and Sam walked through Woodford's peaceful streets and headed out of town along the highway.

Before long, Sam stopped at a big gate. *We're here.*

"This is the old airfield. My dad told me they used to train pilots here." Jennie turned to Sam. "Are you sure this is the place?"

I'm sure. I remember those buildings. A good detective always marks the location.

A chain-link fence with barbed wire on top ran all around the field. Through the fence they could see cement-block buildings, overgrown runways and fields of grass.

Beside the entrance was a small gatehouse. A whiskery face peered out an open window. "Hi, kids! Can I help you?"

With a wide friendly smile, an enormous bearded security guard stepped out. In one hand he held the last bite of a sandwich.

"I'm Fred." He beamed down at them as he stuffed the sandwich into his mouth. "Who are you?"

Sam looked up and up. *Hmm ... I thought of aliens, but I didn't think of giants.*

"I'm Jennie and this is Beth. The dog's name is Sam," answered Jennie. "I dog-sit her."

"You do, huh?" Fred grinned at Sam and scratched behind her ear. "What a nice dog."

Glad you noticed.

Fred looked curiously at the girls. "Are you kids looking for something?"

"Oh no!" said Beth quickly. "We're just out for a walk."

"Not much happening here, is there?" asked

Jennie, trying to start a conversation. "I mean —
no people around."

"Nobody at the moment. I haven't seen
anybody for days."

Well, I've seen somebody.

"Can we go in and look?" asked Beth in her
nicest voice.

Fred shook his huge head. "Afraid not, little
lady. This is a restricted area."

"What does that mean?" Beth looked very
innocent.

"You can't go in. It's off limits." Fred grinned.
"But you can visit me. Want a can of pop?"

Both girls shook their heads. "No, thank you."

*We don't take food from strangers. Do we look
stupid or something?*

"How about a chocolate bar?"

Well ... we might take a chocolate bar.

"No, thank you," said Beth and Jennie
quickly.

One little chocolate bar won't hurt.

Jennie shook her head again. "We'd better be
going."

Just then the gatehouse door opened and another security guard came out. He had a pointy, worried face. "There you are, Fred! It's time to move those boxes."

Fred turned his bulk toward the voice. "This here's Mike. He's my partner." He lowered his voice. "Complains all the time."

Mike stamped his small foot and glared up at his huge partner. "Don't you dare go back to sleep after lunch. I want some help."

Fred sighed. "Some people are so lazy."

"It's not me who's lazy!" Mike's voice rose to a shriek. "This is the fourth time I've moved boxes while you snored."

"Don't listen to him," advised Fred. "The guy's a walking complaint book."

The two security guards started to argue. It seemed that every time there was work to do, Fred went to sleep.

Mike turned on his heels and went back to the gatehouse. The door slammed. Muttering could be heard from inside the door.

Fred sat sadly on a bench. "I don't know why

I get such grumpy partners. My last partner was the biggest grouch I ever met."

Sam chuckled. *I think I know why.*

Then she nudged Jennie's leg. *Ask him some questions, Jennie. Quick — before he goes in.*

"Are you sure we can't look around?" Jennie asked politely.

Beth smiled widely. "We wouldn't touch anything."

"No way," said Fred. "I'd get fired if I let anybody in there."

"Why is it locked up?" Beth asked.

"It's been locked for years," answered Fred, rubbing his whiskers. "We unlocked it last week when a bunch of stuff was delivered. Then we were told to lock it right back up."

Beth was alert. "What kind of stuff?"

Fred made a face. "If you ask me, it was all junk. I hate junk, and I can't see why anybody wants to save it."

Beth did not want to get sidetracked into talking about junk. "Something must happen inside the airfield."

Fred shrugged. "Not much. A fellow used to keep some turkeys in that building over there." He rubbed his whiskers again. "But they were hauled away last week."

So where did they put the delivery stuff?

Jennie cleared her throat. "Excuse me, Fred, but you said a lot of stuff was delivered. Where did they put it?"

"Everything's in that huge building over there. It's the worst garbage you ever saw."

Fred put his hands on his knees and stood up slowly. "Got to get going, kids. It's almost time for lunch." He winked. "Then I'll take my nap."

The three friends watched Fred go into the gatehouse. Shouts and complaints wafted out the open window.

For a few minutes, they stood looking through the wire mesh fence. Before them the silent airfield shimmered in the warm sun.

Quit stalling. Nobody ever solved a mystery by standing at a crummy fence.

"There's no mystery here," muttered Jennie.

"Somebody's using the airfield to store stuff. That's all."

Beth wasn't so sure. "But what about the lights?"

Jennie had no answer.

Slowly the three friends turned and trudged back up the highway toward town.

So what do the deliveries mean? Sam's mind whirred. *Deliveries and elves ... Deliveries and moon-worshiping cults ... Robbers making deliveries ... Witches delivering stuff ... Phooey. Nothing makes sense.*

Then she had a new thought. *Hey! What if aliens are delivering stuff?* She panted, her pink tongue hanging out.

But why would aliens deliver stuff? Sam's mind worked furiously. *Suppose those lights are the aliens landing. Suppose the guys driving the trucks are really aliens in human bodies. Hmm ... The aliens must be getting ready for something ...*

A sudden and terrible thought stopped Sam in her tracks.

They're getting ready to take over Woodford!

6. Everyone Knows about Aliens

All day, Sam thought about aliens. That night she watched out the upstairs window, but there were no lights.

Hmm ... Sometimes they're there and sometimes they're not. I've got to get in that field and find out what's going on. She started to pace.

I'll capture the leader and wreck their plan ... I'll be famous. She saw herself with a little alien on a leash. *I'll take him on all the talk shows. I'll be rich ... I'll be on magazine covers.* She sighed with happiness. *This is fabulous.*

Sam went downstairs and sniffed at the front door. *I wish I could unlock this thing. How can I capture an alien while I'm sitting in here?*

At school, Beth wrote a story about aliens. "It's terrific," said Miss Chong when Beth read it to the class. Beth winked at Jennie.

Beth had written about mysterious lights in a field and how they turned out to be creatures from outer space.

"I like the idea of the lights at night," said Miss Chong, smiling. "Very original, Beth."

"Very original, Beth," Jennie mimicked at recess.

Beth giggled. "I wonder how I thought of it."

Amanda Barnes grabbed Beth's arm. "I saw on TV how aliens take over your body!"

Alec Clarke overheard Amanda. "Hey! I watched that show, too. The aliens get inside you so they can look like a human being."

"Yeah." Amanda's round face grew worried. "They're taking over the whole world – one person at a time."

Jessica Kroger joined the group. "I wonder if we know people who are really aliens."

"I know someone who's an alien!" shouted Josh Keech from behind them. "My brother!"

"It's not a joke, Josh," said Amanda. "Aliens are real."

Alec nodded. "And they look just like you and me."

"You can't tell they're from outer space at all," added Jessica.

"If you see a UFO, call the police." Alec leaned into the group and whispered, "I don't want someone in my family to be an alien."

"It's no use telling the police," scoffed Jessica. "The government already knows and they're hiding it."

"That's what it says in a book Jennie and I are reading!" cried Beth.

"Yeah," added Jennie. "The government keeps loads of secret files about UFOs."

"That's because people would be scared." Alec furrowed his brow. "Everyone would go crazy if they thought their neighbors were aliens."

The little group huddled together and talked while kids pushed and ran and screamed all around them. How could they tell who was an alien?

Jennie and Beth looked at each other. "Do you think Sam's right?" whispered Jennie. "Are aliens planning to take over Woodford?"

"I think Sam's exactly right." Beth's face was grim. "And we have to do something, Jennie. Before it's too late."

7. Sam Has an Idea

Don't tell anybody about the aliens. Sam gobbled the last piece of pizza and licked her chops. *Somebody will try to grab my case. I'm the detective here, and I'm going to be famous.*

"Aliens are dangerous, Sam," objected Jennie.

Forget dangerous. All the good stuff is dangerous.

Jennie sighed. "All Sam cares about is being famous."

"She can't be famous unless we find out something," said Beth. "And I don't know how we're going to find clues."

I know how. Sam fixed Jennie with a hard stare. *If a certain somebody would listen to me.*

Jennie squirmed as Sam stared. "I – I forget what you said."

Beth looked sharply at Jennie. "What did you forget?"

"Nothing … Um … just Sam's idea."

Sam gasped. *You did not forget! Tell Beth I want to sleep in a tent this weekend so we can spy on the airfield.*

"I am not telling Beth," said Jennie.

Sam stared harder. *I'm getting mad.*

"You'd better tell me," giggled Beth. "Sam looks like she's getting angry."

Jennie sighed. "She still wants to go at night. She wants to sleep in a tent so we can get out easily."

"Perfect." Beth jumped up. "I'll ask my mother if we can camp in my backyard."

Jennie looked worried. "It's crazy, Beth. It's dangerous to sneak out in the middle of the night."

"It's the only way to see what the aliens are doing. We'll just have to be careful."

Beth is a lovely kid. Sam glared at Jennie. *Not*

like some wimpy people I could mention.

Now, how about a big piece of cake with some cheese sauce?

On Friday night, Jennie found herself setting up a tent in Beth's backyard.

"I don't like this," Jennie muttered as she laid out her sleeping bag.

Quit complaining. Sam snuffled inside an empty pretzel bag and licked out the salt.

"I'm not complaining." Jennie unpacked pajamas and a flashlight. "I'm scared."

Sam pulled her head out of the bag. *Phooey. I've got great teeth, remember?*

"We have to be careful, Sam."

Trust me.

"Promise you won't do anything dangerous."

Of course not. I've never done anything dangerous in my life.

8. Sleeping in a Tent

THIS WAS A GREAT IDEA!

As twilight settled over Woodford, the backyards grew still. Jennie and Beth lay in their sleeping bags and listened to the last television being switched off and the last door being shut. Darkness surrounded them like velvet.

Jennie's scalp prickled. "I feel as if aliens are all around me."

They are. They're out there getting ready to take over Woodford.

Jennie burrowed into her sleeping bag. "Don't talk about them taking over, Sam."

"I wonder how they take over a person's body?" Beth's eyes peeked out the top of her sleeping bag.

"Remember what Alec said? They zap you and then get inside."

"Oh. Yeah."

Keep your mouth shut so they can't crawl down your throat. That's what I'm going to do.

Jennie hugged her pillow. "Are you sure you want to go out there?"

"It's the only way to see them." Beth gritted her teeth. "We'll go when everyone's asleep."

While they waited, Sam crunched chips and spewed crumbs all over the sleeping bags. She pictured aliens swarming around a spaceship, loading and unloading, getting ready for their attack on Woodford. Chitter. Chitter. Gabble. Gabble. *Wonderful!*

When she finished the chips, she stood up and shook herself. *Let's go. Time for action.*

But Jennie didn't move.

Hey! Get up!

"This is not a good idea, Sam." Jennie's voice was muffled inside her sleeping bag. "It's dangerous for kids to be out at night."

Not when they have a huge sheepdog to protect

them. Sam glared. *I'm getting tired of explaining this.*

Beth thought for a moment. "Maybe it isn't safe for kids to be on the streets so late, Sam. Jennie's probably right."

Okay, okay. Sam sat down with a thud while her mind raced over possibilities. *Here's what we'll do. We'll go through the woods and spy from the back fence.*

"The woods?" Jennie's head popped up.

"Sam's a genius." Beth wriggled out of her sleeping bag and grabbed her flashlight. "Nobody will see us in the woods."

Jennie didn't move.

"Come on, Jennie. We don't have to go on the streets." Beth unzipped Jennie's sleeping bag. "We'll be safe in the woods."

Sam grabbed Jennie's sweatshirt with her teeth and pulled.

Let's go. We're wasting time.

Outside, dark shadows loomed on every side. Without a word, the three friends tiptoed through Beth's garden and out her back gate.

Through the neighbor's yard they crept. Crossing a small street, they entered a dark field. The woods stood before them in jagged black outline against a starry sky.

Jennie gulped.

Relax. My teeth are fabulous.

Together they walked in the rough grass until they came to the edge of the woods.

"Shine your flashlight," whispered Beth.

Both girls flicked on their flashlights and shone the beams into the blackness. Leafy plants and trees stood out in the light. A tiny animal scurried under the leaves. Jennie shuddered.

The three friends stepped into the dark woods. Following Beth's light, they threaded their way through the dense underbrush.

What's this? Disgusting burrs getting stuck in my beautiful fur! Get off me, you sticky little creeps! Go find some ugly dog to stick to.

Hooo-ooo-ooo! An eerie sound filled the woods.

The girls jumped.

Hooo-ooo-ooo-ooo!

Shut up. Now I've got bugs up my nose.

"Maybe it's an owl!" Beth giggled nervously.

Who cares? I've got a stick in my ear.

Hooo-ooo-ooo.

Jennie was too frightened to move. She could feel little eyes watching her from the darkness.

Sam's furry body thumped Jennie's leg. *Quit worrying. We're almost there.* Jennie started moving again.

Suddenly the trees ended. Ahead they could see a grassy space and a high chain-link fence.

"It's the fence around the airfield," whispered Beth, shutting off her flashlight.

Sam went up to the fence and sniffed. *So, where are the aliens?*

The three friends strained to see. But the field was dark and silent.

"Let's wait and see what happens," whispered Beth. Without another word, they sat down in the grass.

All around them echoed small night sounds. A little squeak, a tiny chatter, the hooting of an owl, the harrumph of bullfrogs. Every sound made the girls jump.

There was nothing around them but darkness. They felt as if time had stopped.

Suddenly Sam sat bolt upright. *I hear something!*

She pricked up her ears. *It's them!*

"They're here!" whispered Jennie.

She and Beth covered their heads.

A big beam of light shone out over the field. The aliens had landed!

9. A Nasty Surprise

In the distance Jennie, Beth and Sam heard dull sounds. Thunk. Thunk. For a long time nothing happened. Then the big lights went off and small lights began to pop up all over the field. Each light seemed to stop and look around for a moment. Then it began its strange bobbing rhythm.

Up and down. Down and up. More lights joined the strange pattern.

Jennie, Beth and Sam were still as statues. They couldn't see anything but bouncing lights. It was a scene from another world. Eerie and silent, the dance went on and on.

Listen! They're talking to each other!

Jennie poked Beth. "They're talking!"

The girls strained to listen. Very faintly, they could hear low humming and whistling. Every now and then, a throaty murmur interrupted the whistling.

The guys on TV made a chattering sound. These ones must be from a different planet.

Jennie's scalp prickled. She could imagine the aliens, their antennae waving and their huge eyes rolling as they talked to one another.

Beth gulped. These creatures had traveled from another planet, maybe from another galaxy. And they had come to Woodford. Her throat felt so tight she could hardly breathe.

I wish I understood their language. Then Sam snorted. *It doesn't matter what language they're talking ... I know what they're saying ... Those little creeps are planning to take over.*

The lights danced on and on. Once in a while, a light seemed to look straight at them! Then it started bobbing again.

Sam pressed her face against the fence, pushing the hair away from one eye. But she couldn't see anything except the lights. *This is useless! I have to get in there.*

Jennie grabbed Sam's fur. "We're not going in, Sam! We could get arrested!"

"Never mind being arrested," whispered Beth. "We'll get kidnapped by aliens!"

But Sam wasn't listening. *Great detectives don't sit outside fences. I'm going to catch the leader. I'll keep him in the spare room. Joan and Bob never notice anything.*

Sam imagined taking her captive for a walk. Everyone stopped to congratulate her on saving the town. "The aliens were going to take over Woodford," people cried, "until Sam captured their leader!"

"Sam!" hissed Jennie. "Stop daydreaming! Pay attention! I don't want to get caught!"

Phooey. They're not going to catch us. I'm going to catch one of them.

Sam scratched at the bottom of the fence. *I'll dig my way in. Stay here. I'll be right back.*

"Sam!" cried Jennie. "Stop!"

But Sam didn't stop. Weeds and dirt flew

under her feet.

Suddenly an earsplitting siren tore the still night air.

Eeeee-eeeee-eeeee.

All the lights in the field stopped.

Jennie and Beth clutched each other.

Uh-oh. Sam backed out of the hole.

Eeeee-eeeee-eeeee.

Don't try to wrap me up in a web, you little weirdos. There is a very tough dog here.

Jennie and Beth shook with terror.

The screaming siren split the night air.

Eeeee-eeeee-eeeee.

The lights bobbed into a little group. Then they seemed to turn. Now the lights were coming toward them!

"Oh no!" Jennie's voice cracked.

"Run!" squeaked Beth.

We're out of here!

10. Escape!

Branches whipping their faces, Jennie and Beth floundered in the darkness behind Sam.

They staggered and fell, they bumped into trees, they scraped themselves. But still they crashed on through the night.

Behind them the siren screamed. No one dared look back.

Eeeee-eeeee-eeeee-eeeee-eeeee.

Sweating and scratched, they finally burst out of the woods into the field. In moments they reached the small street behind Beth's house.

All over the neighborhood, porch lights flashed on.

Across the street and through the neighbor's

yard, they streaked. They shot through Beth's back gate and tumbled into the tent.

Eeeee-eeeee-eeeee-eeeee-eeeee.

Sleepy voices sounded from neighboring yards.

Jennie, Beth and Sam burrowed to the bottom of the sleeping bags.

Eeeee-eeeee-eeeee-eeeee-eeeee.

When Beth's father called them from outside the tent door, the girls screamed.

"It's an alien!" yelled Jennie. "It followed us!"

"Bite him, Sam!" hollered Beth.

Sam bared her fangs. "Grrrrr."

Mr. Morrison couldn't hear them over the siren. "Are you kids scared of the noise?"

"Grrrrrr."

"Go away!" shrieked Beth.

"Help!" screamed Jennie. "Help!"

Come right in, you alien creepo. I've got a great set

of teeth waiting for you. "Woof! Woof!"

"What on earth is the matter with you kids?" yelled Beth's dad.

How would you like me to chomp off your antennae? "Woof!"

"Hey, kids!" screeched Beth's father, coming into the tent. "Settle down! The siren's not going to hurt you."

"Eek!" Beth huddled in a little ball with her head in her arms.

"There's nothing to worry about!" screamed Mr. Morrison at the top of his lungs.

Wait a minute! This is no alien.

Jennie poked her head out of her sleeping bag.

"It's not an alien!" Beth yelled. "It's my dad!"

Dashing past Beth's surprised father, Jennie, Beth and Sam shot through the back door of the house and up the stairs.

Mr. Morrison's voice followed them. "You kids have been watching too many movies! The siren won't hurt you!"

"But the aliens will!" shouted Beth from the top of the stairs.

Bursting into Beth's room, they dived into her bed.

The siren stopped. The sudden silence was deafening.

Cowering under Beth's blankets, the three friends watched the window in terror. Any minute, aliens were going to swarm over the glass, looking for the earthlings who had spied on them.

Sam pictured aliens crawling over the window ledge, oozing under the window and flowing over the floor. Chitter. Chitter. Chitter. Up the sides of the bed they crawled, webs spinning out of their long bulbous fingers. Luminous eyes bulged out of their wobbly heads. Gabble. Gabble.

Sam stood up on the bed. "Grrrrrr."

Nobody's wrapping us in a web without a fight!

But nothing came.

The window was dark. The night guarded its mystery in silence.

11. Voices from Another Planet

When the three friends went to Jennie's house the next morning, Mr. Levinsky was sitting at the kitchen table with a new radio. He was turning the dials and muttering.

"Why can't I get a station on this?" he sputtered. "I buy a good short-wave radio, and all I get are whistling noises!"

Sam nudged Jennie's leg. *Whistling! That's what we heard them doing in the field. It's proof the aliens are on the move!*

Jennie's eyes were wide.

Beth gulped. She knew what the whistling meant, too. The aliens were talking to each other and it was blocking the radio signals! "We'd better make some plans," she whispered.

Let's go up to your room. Sam pushed Jennie toward the cupboards. *But we don't want to die of starvation up there, do we?*

Jennie grabbed a huge box of sugarcoated cereal, and they headed upstairs. Jennie shut the door, but they could still hear the radio whistling.

Those whistles sound mad. Sam hopped up on Jennie's bed. *Woodford's in big trouble.*

"Do you really think the aliens will take over?" Jennie sprinkled cereal on the quilt.

Sure. Why else would they come here?

Jennie closed the cereal box slowly. "They wouldn't be here unless they were planning something, right?"

Beth nodded. "Right. We should warn everybody."

Tell Beth not to bother. Nobody listens to kids and dogs.

"Nobody will listen, Beth."

"I know," Beth agreed glumly. "Nobody ever does. But still ..."

Forget it. I'll think of something. Sam lapped up

the cereal and hopped off the bed. *Let's go to the airfield and see what's happening.*

When he saw them, Fred lumbered out of the gatehouse. "You kids should have been here last night! The night shift had some real excitement!"

Jennie tried to look very innocent. "What happened?"

"Somebody set off the alarm!"

"Alarm?" Beth pretended she was only mildly interested.

"It was enough to blast the ears right off your head." Fred peered down at them from under bushy eyebrows. "Didn't you hear it?"

"Uh … Yeah, I guess we did," admitted Jennie.

"We were in bed," added Beth quickly.

Fred took a chocolate bar out of his shirt pocket and ripped off the wrapper. "Something went wrong with the system and they couldn't shut the alarm off."

Hey! It's not polite to eat in front of people!

Fred leaned against the gatehouse. "I'm in big trouble."

"Why are you in trouble?" asked Beth.

"I'm supposed to keep all the systems working. They were perfect when I tested them last week!" Fred scratched his head. "I think somebody's been messing with them."

Sam raised her tufty eyebrows. *And I know who that someone is.*

Fred looked puzzled. "Someone tried to dig under the back fence."

Jennie felt herself getting hot. "Really?"

Sam chortled.

"It's strange." Fred squinted at the gate. "Why would anybody want to get into this old place?"

They've got a reason, Fred. Woodford's in for a big surprise.

How was I supposed to know there was an alarm under the fence? Sam lapped up nachos and licked the inside of the salsa jar.

"Don't dig anywhere else!" cried Jennie. "We're going to get in huge trouble."

Worry. Worry. Fuss. Fuss. Sam snuffled in Jennie's schoolbag. *Where are those gummy worms you had the other day?*

"Forget the gummy worms, Sam. This is serious."

"Yeah." Beth nibbled on a chip. "We can't let aliens take over! We've got to do something!"

Jennie sighed. "We need some adults in on this, don't we?"

Sam pulled her head out of the schoolbag. *Don't tell any adults! We're going to be famous, not them! This is just the kind of thing newspapers love.* She looked in the mirror and turned her head. *Which is my best side for the photographers?*

Jennie looked doubtful. "Don't you think we need help?"

But Sam wasn't listening. She found the gummy worms and chomped happily, the tails of the worms hanging out of her mouth. *We'll save the town ... We'll be heroes. Of course I'll be the main hero. You two will be my assistants ... We'll get medals ... We'll go on talk shows ...*

Sam chewed as she thought. *No. I'll go on the talk shows. You two would hog the camera, and nobody would give me any credit. They'd just say what smart kids you are.*

Sam could feel herself getting angry. *I hate the way humans grab the fame. All they give dogs is a pat on the head. They shout orders at us. They boss us around ...*

Jennie started to giggle. "Sam's getting mad because she thinks we're going to take the credit for saving Woodford."

Beth smiled lovingly at Sam. Then her face clouded. "But we have to save Woodford before anybody can get credit."

That's exactly what I'm going to do. I just have to figure out how.

12. Scary Days

The next few days were frightening. Woodford didn't feel familiar anymore. Neighbors and friends seemed different. Jennie, Beth and Sam looked closely at everyone. It was impossible to tell who was an alien.

Beth thought there was something odd about her mother. Miss Chong started to look very weird. Even Joan and Bob seemed strange.

The nights were long and dark. All three friends slept with one eye on the window, sure that they would see aliens at any moment.

"We can't trust anybody," breathed Jennie.

Don't tell anyone what's happening. You could be telling an alien.

One day the three friends saw four huge transport trucks roll up to the airfield gate. Enormous lumpy things, covered tightly with tarpaulins, were strapped to their flat trailers.

Sam gasped. *Look how big that stuff is! Those are war machines!*

Jennie shivered. Woodford was going to be destroyed, and she didn't know who to trust.

Strange security guards came out to meet the trucks. They didn't smile. They just motioned the trucks through the gate and slammed it shut behind them.

Those guards are aliens! I know it!

Jennie, Beth and Sam watched the trucks rumble over to the biggest building – the one where Fred told them deliveries were stored. For a long time they watched, but nothing happened.

They're waiting until it gets dark. Then they'll take

those tarps off! They don't want anybody to know what they brought.

That night, Sam kept looking out her upstairs window, but the lights never came. In the morning, the trucks were gone and their lumpy cargo was nowhere to be seen.

Ha! Just like I figured. They unloaded the stuff in the middle of the night. I wonder if anyone else noticed.

But everyone on Sam's street was too busy to notice anything. Mrs. Cudmore's dog, Mervin, was missing.

Sam watched Mrs. Cudmore go up and down the street calling for Mervin. "He's been gone for three days," Sam heard her say. "I can't find him anywhere!"

You won't find Mervin, Mrs. Cudmore — unless you're planning to visit outer space.

When Jennie and Beth burst in after school,

they told Sam that Jessica Kroger had lost her cat.

Cat, huh? Those aliens must be desperate.

"Not desperate, Sam. Remember how you thought they'd collect people for their zoo? We think they're collecting animals, too!" Jennie exclaimed.

Beth slumped down on the hall chair. "I hope they don't want too many kids."

Sam gulped. *I bet they want lots of dogs.*

In the middle of the night, Sam paced back and forth. There were no lights in the field again. *They've gone back to their own planet to get something.*

Sam shuddered as she thought about the things aliens might bring back. *Lasers to melt us ... Space beetles to chew us up ... Weird gas to turn us purple ... Big jars to stick us in ... Ugh ... These guys are bad news.*

She went downstairs and found some cake crumbs under the kitchen table. *Ptooh! I hate stale cake.*

Sam paced the kitchen floor. *How can I solve a case when I'm locked in this stupid house?*

Just then a whiff of a breeze ruffled her fur. Sam stopped and looked around. The patio door was open!

Sam pushed sideways with her paw. The screen slid back. Sam was out!

Yes! Another brilliant move by a great detective!

Sam sat on the back deck and looked up at the stars. Across the diamond-studded sky, a little white light bleeped. *There they go with Mrs. Cudmore's dog — and Jessica Kroger's cat.*

I wonder who they'll grab next ... Sam's mind ran over all the cats she would like to get rid of, all the bossy people who should get zapped.

Then a terrible thought made her blood run cold. *What if aliens grab Jennie or Beth? Uh-oh ... There's no time to waste.*

Sam slipped out of her backyard and padded down the empty street. All the houses were dark. She crossed Main Street and headed out to the highway.

Whoosh. Whoosh. Trucks zipped by. No one was interested in a dog on the side of the road.

Sam turned into the blackness of the old airfield. She nosed up and down the fence, sniffing and listening. Nothing was happening. No lights. No spaceships. No people.

Sam squinted at the gatehouse. *So where are the security guards?*

Just then a bright beam of light swept over the driveway. Sam leaped behind a bush. A truck pulled up. *Aliens!*

The driver hopped out and punched some buttons on the fence. The gate slid open. Then he jumped back behind the wheel and roared through.

This is too good to miss! Like a shot, Sam dashed for the open gate.

Just as it was closing, she squeezed in. The truck drove off ahead.

Sam was inside the airfield.

13. Trapped!

Listening and sniffing, Sam nosed around the dark airfield. *There have to be some clues here.*

In the distance Sam heard the truck doors slam. *Here come the weapons.* She thought of the space battles she'd seen on TV. *People zapped into a thousand pieces. Melted into a puddle. Beamed up to another planet ...*

I have to see their weapons. She headed toward the sounds. Crossing the field, she crept up to the big building and crouched in the shadows. She could hear thumping and bumping.

"Careful," muttered a gravelly voice. "If this gets broken, we're in big trouble."

"If you ask me, this stuff's already broken,"

grumbled another voice.

Thud. Thud. Footsteps.

Sam listened to doors opening and closing. She caught a faint whiff of aftershave.

If they're moving equipment in the dead of night, the attack's going to be a surprise. People will think it's an ordinary day, then ... ZAP! The aliens will attack and Woodford will be finished.

Sam was deep in thought when a bright beam of light blinded her.

She blinked. *Uh-oh!*

"What's this!" roared the gravely voice.

"Looks like a dog!"

"I can see it's a dog. Grab it!"

Sam bolted, but arms as strong as iron shot out of the darkness and grabbed her fur. A light shone into her eyes so she couldn't see.

Snarling and squirming, Sam snapped wildly at her attackers. *These guys have twenty arms!*

"Hey!" said the first voice. "I saw this dog hanging around the other night!" A strong hand clamped on to Sam's collar.

Well I'm not hanging around now! Sam twisted

and tried to bite. She pulled her head backward out of her collar. *I'm out of here! I'm a very tough dog.* "Grrrrrr."

Suddenly a rope jerked over Sam's head. She bucked like a bronco but the rope pulled tight.

She felt herself being lifted off the ground and heaved into the air. With a thump, she landed on a hard floor. *Oh, no! The spaceship!*

Doors clanged shut, and Sam was plunged into blackness.

They're taking me to their planet!

The spaceship moved. In the oily-smelling darkness, Sam bounced around uncomfortably. After a very long time, the movement stopped. When the doors flew open, Sam was blinded by blazing light again.

"You're here, mutt," said a voice from the brightness. "This is your new home."

Strong hands lifted Sam. She couldn't see

anything but searing light.

Snarling and growling, Sam was pulled down a long hallway. She stiffened and scratched the floor with her toenails. Terrified barks and woofs and yelps echoed around her.

Her jailer stopped at a small door. Sam tried to writhe out of his grasp. *I'm going to bite this guy's foot off!*

But Sam was shoved inside. Clang! The door banged shut.

Gradually, Sam's eyes adjusted to the darkness, and she could see she was in a cage. She smelled dogs all around her, but she couldn't see them.

Sam pricked up her ears and listened to their sorrowful whining. *There are a million dogs in here.*

Her heart sank. *No wonder they're sad. The aliens are collecting us for their crummy zoo.*

Sam stood up. "Woof!" *Hey, guys!*

Sam sent out her thoughts as hard as she could. *Hello-o!*

She scrunched up her eyes and tried harder.

Hey! I'm talking to you! "Woof! Woof!"

But the whines and yelps went on.

Sam called and called. *Hello! Hey, you guys! Listen to me! Hello! What's the matter? Are you all deaf?*

But there was no answer.

With a thud, Sam flopped to the cement floor. *So ... they only kidnap stupid dogs. Well, they made a big mistake with me.*

As time passed, the horror of being in the alien zoo dawned on Sam. *No snacks. No friends. No adventure. Geeky aliens gawking at me. Stupid dogs who don't understand a word I say ...*

I've got to get out of here.

Joan banged on Jennie's back door the next morning. "Our patio door is open! Sam's disappeared!"

When Jennie's parents rushed outside to look, Jennie picked up the phone. "Beth, the aliens have taken Sam! Joan's patio door was open this morning, and Sam's gone!"

Everyone searched for Sam. "First, poor little Mervin and now Sam!" said Jennie's mother. "What's going on?"

"And Jessica Kroger's cat," added Jennie.

"Poor Sam," sniffled Beth.

After searching all day, Beth stayed with Jennie, but neither of them could sleep. White-faced and frightened, they talked about what the aliens would do next.

"How could they kidnap Sam inside her own house?" Jennie asked.

"They have special powers," Beth answered glumly. "They can see everything."

Jennie looked around the room. "Maybe they can see through w-walls."

"I bet they're watching us right now." Beth's face was pale.

Jennie's brown hair was wild and her face was blotchy. "How will we get Sam back?"

Beth chewed her fingernails in silence. Tears welled up in her green eyes. "What if they've taken her to their planet?"

Jennie looked out at the night sky. Dark clouds huddled over the rooftops. The aliens were out there, traveling from star to star. And somewhere in the vastness of space, Sam was frightened and alone.

"I can hear her, Beth," cried Jennie. "Sam's calling me!"

14. The Worst Days of Sam's Life

When Beth and Jennie opened their eyes at 5:30 the next morning, they were instantly awake.

"Let's look for Sam again," Beth whispered. "Nobody checked the airfield."

Jennie hopped out of bed.

Quietly they crept through the sleeping house and let themselves out. Jennie closed the front door with a tiny click.

In the dim early-morning light, the streets were gray and silent. Past Sam's house and down Main Street they walked. Their skin crawled and their hearts pounded. An alien could swoop out of the sky and grab them at any moment.

As they headed out of town along the edge of the highway, Jennie spoke at last. "I – I don't think she's out here."

"I think the aliens have taken her someplace." Beth looked around nervously.

"She's calling me. But I d-don't know what to do –" Jennie's voice faltered.

The old airfield was deserted. Jennie and Beth looked helplessly at the gate.

Jennie felt her scalp prickle. "I – I hope the aliens aren't hiding here," she whispered.

Beth peered in the dusty windows of the empty gatehouse. "There's nobody here, Jennie."

Jennie twisted her hands with worry. "Sam's calling me, Beth. But her voice is getting fainter. What are we going to do?"

After school, Jennie and Beth went to Sam's house. Joan was in the kitchen crying. "I've called everyone I know," she sobbed. "Nobody's seen Sam!"

Jennie and Beth felt their hearts sink.

Just then the doorbell rang. Jennie's father poked his head in the door. "I think I've found her!" he cried.

"Where is she?" they all shouted.

"You won't believe it," said Mr. Levinsky. "There's a sheepdog in the pound with no collar. It might be Sam! That could explain why they didn't have Sam's tag number when we called yesterday."

"The pound!" screeched Beth.

Jennie's hand flew to her mouth. "Sam will be furious!"

Joan slumped on a chair. "But Sam always wears her collar," she muttered, puzzled. "Besides, how could she end up in the dog pound? When we went to bed, she was here!"

Jennie's dad said he'd go to see if it was Sam. Jennie and Beth jumped in the car with him.

The girls fidgeted during the long drive to the animal shelter. When they got there, it seemed to take forever before the forms were filled out and a woman led them down a long cement hall. Mournful whines and sorrowful barking filled the air.

In her head, Jennie could hear Sam's voice getting louder as she walked. *Hurry up, Jennie. I'm hungry and these stupid dogs are all deaf. Come and get me.*

Walking faster, Jennie yelled, "I'm coming, Sam!" The woman gave Jennie an odd look.

At last they stopped in front of a small door. When the woman opened it, out burst a white tornado! It slobbered all over them!

"SAM!" Jennie and Beth laughed and cried and hugged Sam.

"I heard you calling!" Jennie buried her face in Sam's fur.

I thought you were as deaf as these dogs!

Sam was suddenly huffy. *I called you day and night. I'm thirsty and I'm starving. I've got a broken neck and I'm in a bad mood.*

"Aren't you glad to see us?" Jennie stroked the big dog lovingly.

Sam slurped at Jennie's face. *Of course I'm glad — but I had a very rough time.*

Jennie hugged Sam with all her strength. "It was the worst two days of my life."

"Mine, too," added Beth.

Sam snorted. *Never mind your life. It was the worst two days of my life!* She looked around curiously.

So ... tell me where I am.

15. What Happened to Sam

I've never been so humiliated in my life!

Sam sputtered as she gobbled the last piece of apple pie. She sidled over to the bowl of root beer and took a few noisy slurps. *Imagine me locked up with riffraff. Dog criminals ... dogs with fleas ... dogs who fight. Me! A famous detective shoved in the dog pound with scuzzos!*

Sam sat down and scratched furiously. Tufts of hair flew around the room. *This is revolting. I think I caught fleas from those lowlifes!*

"Sam thinks she's got fleas," Jennie giggled. "She also thinks the dog pound is beneath her dignity."

Beth laughed until her red hair bounced

merrily. "It's a dog pound, Sam! It's for dogs."

Sam fixed Beth with a terrible look. *Tell this kid I'm no ordinary dog, Jennie. I'm clever. I'm talented and I'm famous — at least I will be famous when I get my paws on an alien. I don't associate with riffraff.*

Sam climbed up on the bed and looked around grumpily. *I'm out of food. I've been starving for two days, remember?*

"What would you like to eat now, Sam?" Beth giggled.

Sam glared at Jennie. *Cheese strings with chocolate sauce and ketchup would be nice. And some butter tarts — watermelon — buttered raisin toast — pizza — a few tacos.*

"Coming right up." Jennie left the room, laughing. Sam turned her scowl on Beth. Then she lifted her back leg and scratched fiercely behind one ear.

"Don't be so mad, Sam," said Beth gently. "It was only a dog pound. Lots of dogs go there sooner or later."

Sam scratched harder. *A person like me does not belong in a dog pound.*

Jennie burst back in the bedroom with a tray. "Cheese strings, ketchup, frozen butter tarts. We don't have watermelon or chocolate sauce, so I brought barbecue chips." She bowed. "Here you are, Your Majesty."

Very funny. Sam sniffed and scratched wildly. *Since you think it's hilarious, I'll put some fleas in your bed.*

"Sam's in a very bad mood." Jennie winked at Beth. "But she's had a terrible time, so it's not her fault."

Beth made her face look very sad. "Of course it's not. There's nothing funny about being stuck in a dog pound. Sam was really brave."

Hmph. That's better. Sam gulped down two butter tarts. *A little ketchup would be good on these.*

Jennie poured ketchup over the remaining tarts. Sam polished the food off and burped.

Then she stretched out on the bed. *I feel a bit better.*

"Now." Jennie leaned forward. "Tell us how you got in the dog pound."

Sam raised her big head. *I was grabbed. There I was, minding my own business. Just trying to solve a mystery like any good detective when ... Wham! A bunch of aliens threw me in their spaceship and dumped me in the dog pound. I thought they were taking me to their zoo.*

Jennie gasped. "Aliens grabbed you? Right in your own house?"

Well ... not exactly.

Jennie squinted at Sam.

Joan and Bob left the patio door open. All I had to do was push the screen a bit.

Jennie was shocked. "Sam wasn't stolen, Beth! She pushed the screen door open!"

Beth looked puzzled. "Where did the aliens get her?"

Jennie stood up. "Sam! Were you out on the street?"

Uh ... Not exactly ... I was sort of ... inside the airfield.

"Inside the airfield!" Jennie shrieked. "With aliens landing there! You're crazy!"

No need to be insulting.

"How did she get in?" Beth asked.

A truck went in.

"And you sneaked in behind the truck!" Jennie was furious.

Well, sort of.

"What did the spaceship look like?"

Dark. They didn't want me to see anything so they shone a light in my eyes.

Sam sat up. *Never mind that stuff. Guess who was driving the truck?*

"Who?" Jennie was curious.

Some grumpy security guards we don't know.

"So?"

So — when they grabbed me, they were stronger than normal people. They had loads of arms. Those guys were aliens, Jennie!

Sam paused. *Remember Fred and Mike?*

"Yeah."

They weren't there. The aliens must have zapped them. By now they've taken over their bodies!

"Tell me! Tell me!" cried Beth, her green eyes blazing with curiosity.

When Jennie had repeated what Sam said,

Beth paled. "How are we going to get anybody to help us?"

We don't need help. Woodford is lucky I'm such a smart detective. Otherwise we'd all be zapped into outer space while we're sleeping. Or we'd have creepy little aliens crawling down our throats.

Sam held her head proudly. *All I have to do is grab the leader. I can't wait to be famous.*

Fame is good.

16. We Have to Trick Them

After everyone was asleep that night, Sam watched from the upstairs window. Lights! Up and down. Down and up. In silence the aliens went about their work.

The next day, two more transport trucks rumbled through town and went out to the old airfield. Their lumpy cargo was covered with tightly strapped tarpaulins. It was impossible to see what was underneath.

Sam watched the trucks in disgust. *See how these crummy aliens work? First they take over some human bodies. Then they bring in a ton of weapons to finish off the rest of us.*

"Yeah," muttered Jennie. "What can two kids

and a dog do against a zillion aliens?"

We need a trick. Hmmm ...

Just leave it to me.

Jennie and Beth went back to the library to get more information about aliens. There were shelves and shelves of books. They each took an armful back to Jennie's room.

Sam climbed on the bed and grumbled. *If I have to put up with all this reading, I want a giant bag of cheese puffs. And a jumbo bottle of pop.*

Jennie sighed. "We'll have to get her some snacks, Beth. Otherwise she'll bug us while we read."

Beth giggled. "I bet she wants pickled herring with ice cream and ketchup."

That sounds good.

Jennie and Beth put their money together, ran to the corner store and bought cheese puffs and red pop. Then they settled down to read.

Sam's chomping and slurping were the only sounds in the room.

"This is worse than I thought," said Jennie grimly. "Aliens have all sorts of special powers."

Beth's fluffy head was bent low over her book. "This book says they can hear what we're thinking!"

Then they know I think they're creeps and weirdos.

"Aliens have mind control, Beth!" Jennie pointed to a page. "You get an idea and you think it's your own – but an alien is really telling you what to do."

"We can guard against that," Beth said firmly.

"How?"

"If we get an idea that helps the aliens, we'll know it's mind control. So we won't do it." Beth went back to her book, but a moment later she shrieked. "This book says aliens come to Earth to make us slaves!"

Sam shuddered. She could see herself harnessed to a cart, pulling a heavy load. Little creatures thronged around her, waving their antennae. Chitter. Chitter. Gabble. Gabble.

Whips flashed over her back. There was no food in sight.

Sam shook her big head. *Whew! They're not taking me prisoner without a fight.*

"What can we do?" Jennie looked worried. "We can't stop an army of aliens."

We're smarter than them. We'll trick them into going home.

"Trick them?"

Beth chewed her fingernails. "How can you fool aliens?"

Tell them there's a big disease on Earth. If they don't get away fast, they'll catch it.

"Sam thinks we should warn them there's a bad disease here. Then they'll leave."

"Wow! Smart dog, Sam." Beth patted Sam's furry head.

Sam sniffed. *I hate it when people are surprised by my brilliance.*

So . . . what are we waiting for?

17. The Aliens' Secret Weapon

After school the next day, Jennie, Beth and Sam walked to the old airfield.

With a friendly wave, Fred lumbered out of the gatehouse.

Watch it everybody! This is no longer a nice guy with a chocolate bar. Underneath he's got six heads, buggy eyes and crawly antennae.

"H-hello," stammered Jennie.

"Hi there!" sang Beth in a cheerful voice.

"How are you kids doing?" boomed Fred. "I haven't seen you for a while."

"I-I-I guess we've been busy," stuttered Jennie. She looked closely at Fred. He seemed different.

"Busy!" Fred threw out his huge hands. "You

should work here! There's so much going on, I can't stand it!"

Sam squinted suspiciously up at Fred's whiskery face. *Ask him why he's so busy.*

"W-what's making you so busy?"

"Yeah," chimed in Beth. "We saw a lot of trucks coming in here."

"The big event is this weekend, little lady!" answered Fred. "Don't forget to come."

As if we'd do what you tell us, you crummy alien.

"B-b-big event?" Jennie watched him closely.

"What's happening?" Beth tried to look innocent.

Fred winked. "Be here on Saturday morning. Eleven o'clock. You'll see."

We don't listen to weirdos from other planets. Go back to your own galaxy.

Fred waggled a huge finger. "Yup. Saturday's going to be a big day around here."

Forget this Saturday business. Tell him about the disease.

Jennie cleared her throat. "A lot of people in town are getting sick – with a very bad flu."

"Yeah," added Beth, her eyes wide, "we heard it can kill you in three days."

Fred rubbed his whiskers. "I hate the flu."

Good. So go home and don't bother us.

Jennie tried to look wise. "A lot of our neighbors are sick."

Tell him they're dying! Sick doesn't sound scary enough.

"People are dying!" cried Jennie suddenly.

Fred's eyebrows shot up. "You don't say?"

We do say. So hop in your spaceship and buzz off.

"I'll be very careful about this flu," said Fred.

The strange way he was looking at them made Sam uncomfortable. She watched him carefully. Then she knew. *Uh-oh.*

Sam nudged Jennie's leg. *We'll say good-bye now. Heh. Heh. It's been lovely chatting with you, Fred. What a nice guy you are. You don't look at all like an alien.*

She bumped Jennie harder. *Time to go! Keep up the good work, Fred. Always wanted to be a security guard myself. Love the uniform. La-la-la-la-la-la ... Got to go ... La-la.*

Jennie was bewildered. "W-well, I guess we'd better be going."

Fred looked puzzled. "Okay. See you later. Don't forget about Saturday."

Without waiting another second, Sam trotted quickly along the edge of the road toward town.

Jennie and Beth hurried after her.

Sam didn't look back. *Whew! That was close!*

"What's wrong, Sam?" Jennie called.

But Sam kept heading toward Woodford. When she got to Main Street, she stopped and waited for Jennie and Beth to catch up.

"What's the matter, Sam?" panted Jennie.

You can't lie to those guys!

Jennie was surprised. "Why not?"

Didn't you notice?

"Notice what?"

An alien has taken over Fred's body, Jennie.

Jennie nodded. "I know. So?"

So, think. Sam looked hard at Jennie.

That guy was reading our minds!

18. A Great Thing for Woodford

THAT'S WHAT THEY THINK!

"It's a great thing for Woodford!" said Jennie's mother at dinner that night.

Noel was sulky. "What's the big deal?"

"I'll tell you what the big deal is," said their father. "Woodford's getting a new museum."

"Who cares?" Noel stuffed half a grilled-cheese sandwich into his mouth.

"We care." Mr. Levinsky was firm. "A new museum is a wonderful thing, and we're all going to the grand opening."

Jennie was bored. "Where's the museum going to be?" she asked idly.

"At the old airfield." Mrs. Levinsky passed the sandwiches.

Jennie looked up in surprise.

"I think it's the perfect spot." Jennie's mother smiled. "That place has been empty for years."

Jennie was suddenly very interested. "They're turning the old airfield into a museum?"

Her mother nodded. "An airplane museum. It's going to be really interesting."

Jennie's head was spinning. Something was wrong.

"I'm not interested," Noel muttered. "It sounds boring."

"You might be surprised," answered their mother. "The museum is opening on Saturday. You'll learn a lot about the history of flight."

Jennie's mind whirled. Aliens were in control of the airfield! Fred said that Saturday was the big day, but Fred is an alien. What will happen when people go there?

Jennie gobbled the last bite of her sandwich and excused herself.

She had to see Sam and Beth.

Half an hour later, the three friends were shut in Jennie's bedroom.

I know what those creeps are doing. Sam sat on the bed chewing a long string of red licorice.

"What?"

You aren't going to like this. It's very scary.

"Scary?"

"What's Sam talking about?" Beth threw down a book on UFOs.

She isn't going to like it either.

"So tell us." Jennie looked worried.

Well – Sam burped loudly. *Are you ready?*

"We've been ready for hours," cried Jennie. "Tell us!"

The whole town is going to the museum opening on Saturday, right?

Jennie nodded. "Right."

That's no accident. Sam's pink tongue hung out. *When everyone gets to the airfield, what do you think the aliens are going to do?*

"Zap us!" screamed Jennie.

"Zap us?" shrieked Beth. "What's Sam saying?"

"Sam thinks the aliens want everybody at the

airfield," Jennie explained.

"I get it!" Beth gasped. "Then they can zap the whole town at once."

Sam nodded. *They'll send a huge spaceship. Then they'll open those big doors like I saw on TV. They'll send out rays and . . . Whoosh! We're toast.*

Jennie gulped. "All the people in Woodford will be sucked up and whisked away to outer space."

Beth's eyes were huge. "We don't stand a chance."

The hair over Sam's eyes moved up and down calmly. *Don't worry. I'll save everybody.*

"Yeah, right." Jennie rolled her eyes. "One dog can save a whole town."

Beth was not impressed. "How's she going to do that?"

But Sam wasn't listening. *The whole world will send reporters to Woodford. Talk shows. Interviews. A movie contract. I'll charge a million dollars a movie! Sam, the famous dog who saved the planet . . .*

Jennie sighed. "Stop daydreaming, Sam."

Beth looked grim. "We need a plan."

19. Sam Needs an Idea

DON'T RUSH ME. I'M THINKING.

From the upstairs window, Sam watched trucks roll into the airfield by day. Then, at night the lights appeared. Night after night the aliens landed and unloaded their weapons.

Sam was shocked. *How much stuff do these guys need?*

Each day brought Saturday closer. Jennie and Beth started to panic.

Quit worrying. If the aliens need this much equipment, they must be wimps.

"We have to think of a plan, Sam," Jennie said desperately. "Tomorrow is Saturday!"

Don't rush me. Brainy people need peace and quiet to be creative. Sam chomped peanut butter cookies. Crumbs spewed out the sides of her mouth.

Beth bit her fingernails furiously. "We have to warn our parents."

Big waste of time. Remember? Nobody listens to kids and dogs.

But Jennie was nodding at Beth, her eyes wide and frightened. When she spoke, her voice was low. "Somebody has to tell them. Tomorrow is our last day on Earth."

Jennie's father thought she was joking. "This is ridiculous! The whole family is going to the museum opening tomorrow, and that's final."

"But the security guards are aliens, Dad!" cried Jennie.

"Nonsense!" said her mother. "You've been watching too much television."

"I saw little green men on the roof yesterday, Jennie." Noel doubled over with laughter. "I think they were friends of yours."

"Now, Jennie." Her father was trying to be patient. "Don't you think you're being just a little silly? There are no aliens."

Jennie sighed. Sam was right. No one was listening.

Sam was sympathetic. *Don't feel bad, Jennie. Nobody appreciates my intelligence either.*

Beth was miserable. "My family thinks I'm nuts!"

Forget about it. I'll think of something.

"We need an idea, Sam!" Jennie's brown eyes clouded. "Tomorrow we're all going to be zapped!"

Don't rush me. I'll come up with a great idea.

Sam nudged Jennie gently with her nose. *You'll see.*

20. Sam Figures It Out

Saturday morning dawned like any other Saturday. The Levinskys got ready to go to the ceremony. No one realized this was their last day on the planet.

"Hurry up, Jennie," her mother called from the kitchen.

Slowly Jennie pulled on her jeans. She felt sick. Woodford was doomed.

At the airfield, the big gate was open and flags were flying from the gatehouse. As Jennie's family pulled into the parking lot, Jennie saw Beth getting out of the Morrisons' car. Her little brothers tumbled out happily, but Beth looked pale and worried.

Joan and Bob pulled up with Sam in the back seat. They parked next to the Levinskys, and the three families walked together.

"What a lovely day!" remarked Jennie's mother as they sat down in a row of chairs.

You won't think it's so lovely when you're in outer space. Sam wedged herself between Jennie and Beth.

A platform was decorated with flowers and lined with chairs for special guests. Security guards were everywhere.

All these aliens make me nervous. Sam leaned against Jennie's knee and muttered, *Look at these creeps, strutting around, pretending they're human. Don't let them take over your body. Keep your mouth shut.*

Jennie elbowed Beth. "Keep your mouth closed."

Beth clamped her teeth together.

Jennie leaned down to Sam. "Have you thought of anything yet?"

I'm working on it.

Beth chewed her fingernails. "This is making

me very nervous."

Anxiously, Jennie and Beth looked up for signs of a spaceship. Nothing marred the empty blue sky.

No point looking. When it comes, it'll zoom in so fast we won't even see it.

Sam fidgeted. *I wish I had a snack. Stress always makes me hungry.*

It seemed like hours before the ceremony got started.

Finally, special guests filed up to the stage. A man tapped the microphone and made a long boring speech about the new museum. People clapped. Then more people made speeches. Their voices droned on and on.

The aliens were lined up on both sides of the platform. They looked like ordinary security guards. Fred kept winking at Jennie, Beth and Sam.

Sam turned her head away. *What a big phony he is. Don't look at him.*

Some people lined up and cut a big ribbon. Everyone clapped and clapped. Some lady talked and talked. In spite of their fears, Jennie and Beth felt as if they were going to fall off their chairs with boredom.

At last Sam nudged Jennie. *I've figured it out. I know what to do.*

Jennie leaned toward Beth excitedly. "Sam's got her idea!"

Remember that book where the army stopped the aliens with foam? Jennie nodded. The hair over Sam's eyes rose and fell. *Remember how the aliens got stuck in it?*

Jennie nodded.

So, I need to turn on that fire hose. Sam jerked her head at the fire emergency stand at the side. There were two hoses, one with a picture of water on it and the other with a picture of foam. *You and Beth come with me. I'll spray this whole place with foam.*

Jennie gasped. "Sam's going to spray

everybody with foam from that fire hose!"

"Oh no!" Beth looked horrified.

"We can't do that!" whispered Jennie. "I'd be grounded forever!"

Hurry up. Sam bumped both their legs with her round black nose. *We don't have time to waste. A spaceship could land any minute!*

"We're not doing that, Sam!"

Yes, we are. Sam stood up and tried to squeeze past Jennie.

"No way!" Jennie stuck out her legs to block Sam.

Beth grabbed Jennie's arm. "Sam's right. We have to do it!" She swallowed hard. "I don't care how much I get punished. We have to save everybody."

Jennie stiffened her legs as Sam pushed. "My parents would go crazy!"

"We don't have any choice." Beth stuck out her chin bravely. "I'll help you, Sam," she whispered.

I told you Beth was a lovely kid. Sam shoved harder against Jennie's legs. *Get out of my way. Or I'll bite.*

"Shhhh!" hissed people behind them. "We can't hear the speeches."

"Be quiet over there!" snapped a lady crossly.

Sam glared up at everyone. *Tell those crabby people we're trying to save them.*

Jennie shrank down in her chair. Her face turned bright red.

Sam bumped Jennie's legs so hard she broke through. She started to shove past the people in the row. *Come on, Jennie. Tell your mother you have to go to the washroom.*

But Jennie didn't move.

Beth jumped up to follow Sam. Jennie grabbed Beth's skirt. "Stay here! We'll get in huge trouble!"

Sam whirled around and glared at Jennie. *Who cares about trouble? We're saving a whole town here. I'm going to be a big hero.*

"Darn kids," muttered a man in a dark blue suit.

"Who brought that stupid-looking dog anyway?" complained a woman with dangling earrings.

"Don't people teach their children how to behave!" exclaimed a crabby-looking man.

Mr. and Mrs. Morrison glared at Beth. Mr. and Mrs. Levinsky glared at Jennie. Joan and Bob reached out to grab Sam, but she was too fast for them. With Beth behind her, Sam shoved past person after person.

Grumbles and mutters and groans echoed up and down the row.

"Sit down!" ordered a woman whose three perfect children sat with their hands folded.

"That red-headed kid is a brat!" snarled a man in a golf shirt. His son looked as if he wanted to shrink inside his clothes.

"Children today are monsters," twittered a sweet old lady. "Absolute monsters."

Beth flushed beet red, but she didn't stop. When they got to the end of the row, Sam and Beth trotted straight to the fire box. With a quick movement, Beth slid back the latch that locked the door.

Sam grabbed the fire-hose nozzle with her wonderful teeth and started to run.

21. Sam's Big Mistake

SO ... NOBODY'S PERFECT.

Jennie felt as if she was going to explode. Sam marched up the side of the crowd with the fire-hose nozzle in her mouth. Then she stopped and aimed it at the crowd!

Joan looked too horrified to move. The speeches from the platform droned on. Nobody else had noticed Sam.

Jennie looked overhead to see if there was a spaceship coming. But the wide blue sky gleamed emptily.

She heard Bob muttering, "Wait until I get my hands on that dog, Joan. She's going to obedience school and that's final!"

Mrs. Morrison let out a little gasp. "If Beth

doesn't come back this minute, she's going to be grounded for a month!"

At that moment, a strange-looking group of people climbed the side stairs and lined up across the platform. They wore hats with lights on them, and were dressed in white coveralls that had 'Fenwicks Dew Worms' sewn on the front.

Fear slithered through Jennie. Maybe the aliens were not going to land a spaceship. Maybe all of them were already here!

Jennie tried to catch Sam's eye. Frantically she pointed at the stage.

Sam saw Jennie pointing and looked up at the stage. *Who cares about a bunch of hospital workers? They don't have anything to do with this.* Sam turned back to the audience and aimed the nozzle again. *Tell Beth to turn this thing on!*

One of the men walked over to the microphone and shook the mayor's hand.

"We owe Fenwicks a great big thank you," the mayor said.

Hey! The fire hose, remember?

But Jennie was listening to the mayor. Beth watched the stage closely, a surprised look spreading over her face.

"Has anybody noticed strange lights here at night?" the mayor asked.

The crowd nodded.

"Well, here's the reason for those mysterious lights!" The mayor laughed. "You've been seeing the lights on their hats!"

Jennie and Beth looked at each other in horror.

What's the matter with you, Jennie? Get Beth to turn this thing on! I'm trying to save us here! Work with me!

"As some of you know," continued the mayor, "Fenwicks has had the contract to pick worms at the airfield this year."

The crowd clapped. The Fenwicks people bowed.

"And that money has helped start this aircraft museum!" The mayor clapped heartily.

The crowd cheered. The Fenwicks people bowed again.

"Tell me truthfully." The mayor grinned. "Wasn't anybody worried about those lights at night?"

Sam's head whipped around. The nozzle hung out of her mouth. *Wait a minute!* She looked at the mayor. She looked at the Fenwicks people. She looked at their hats. *Uh-oh.*

One of the worm pickers made a speech. The audience clapped and clapped.

Jennie and Beth locked eyes across the sea of heads. Worm pickers! Those were the lights they saw!

Sam dropped the fire hose and tried to crawl under an empty chair.

I'll never hear the end of this.

22. Not My Fault

HOW WAS I SUPPOSED TO KNOW?

In Jennie's bedroom that night, Jennie and Beth glared at Sam.

So I was a little wrong. Sam sniffed. *Nobody's perfect.*

"You were a lot wrong!" yelled Jennie. "You were about to spray everybody with foam, you bad dog! The whole town would have hated us!"

Watch who you're calling bad. I feel like biting somebody.

"What would have happened to us if we'd sprayed everyone?" Beth groaned and fell on the bed. "I'd be locked in my room for a year!"

Sam raised her chin haughtily. *We were trying to help them. People should appreciate it.*

"Noel is laughing like a hyena because we thought worm pickers were aliens." Jennie sighed. "He's never going to shut up about it."

Let him laugh. He's a big teenage lummox, and I hate teenagers.

"Aliens didn't grab Mrs. Cudmore's dog – or Jessica Kroger's cat. They've been found." Jennie held her head in her hands. "Noel's laughing his head off about that, too!

Beth was glum. "I asked my parents about worm picking. They said people put lights on their hats so they can see the worms."

"Why don't they pick worms during the day? Then they wouldn't need lights."

"They have to do it at night, when the dew is on the ground. That's when worms come out of their holes."

Hmph. So why do they only work some nights?

Jennie rolled over on her stomach and put her head on her arms. "Why don't they come every night, Beth?"

"Some nights there's no dew, so the worms just stay in their holes."

"I guess that's why they're called dew worms," Jennie said sadly.

Sam sniffed. *Hmph. Well, how was I supposed to know all that?*

Jennie eyed Sam with exasperation. "You sure get us in a lot of trouble, Sam."

At least I'm not boring.

Sam nuzzled under the bed and dragged out a bag of chips. *Lucky I knew these were here. You'd probably get crabby if I asked for a snack right now.*

She stuck her nose in the bag and started to munch. Chips dribbled on to the floor.

It's not my fault those worm pickers looked like aliens ... Besides, they had no right to act sneaky.

She gobbled another mouthful of chips and looked around happily.

Ah, that's better.

Now ... is there anything else going on in this town that I should know about?

Enter our
Sam: Dog Detective Draw

The Grand Prize winner will receive a 28" adorable plush sheepdog along with a complete collection of Sam: Dog Detective books, signed by the author. Two second-prize winners will receive the signed book collection as well as an 11" plush sheepdog. Ten third-prize winners will receive the complete collection of Sam: Dog Detective books, signed by the author.

Here's how it works. To enter the draw, write a short adventure story (less than 200 words) about a real or make-believe dog. Send us your story along with your name, address, age and home phone number.

Residents of Canada:	Residents of the United States:
Sam: Dog Detective Contest	Sam: Dog Detective Contest
c/o Kids Can Press	c/o Kids Can Press
29 Birch Avenue	4500 Witmer Estates
Toronto, Ontario	Niagara Falls, NY
M4V 1E2	14305-1386

SPYING ON DRACULA

Sam, Dog Detective, sniffs out adventure!

Ten-year-old Jennie Levinsky has a secret – and only her best friend, Beth, knows about it. Jennie can "hear" what her neighbor's sheepdog, Sam, is thinking! And what Sam is thinking leads the girls into an exciting adventure at the spookiest house in town. Why is the house always dark? Why is a bat always hanging around? And who is that frightening creature living inside? Sam comes to the only logical conclusion – Dracula lives there!

THE GHOST OF CAPTAIN BRIGGS

Sam, Dog Detective, digs up a mystery!

Jennie and Beth are all set to enjoy their summer vacation with Sam. But how could they know that the house Jennie's family has rented was built long ago by a bloodthirsty pirate? Sam convinces Jennie that where there's a pirate, there must be buried treasure ... and a ghost guarding it. What else could explain the spooky housekeeper, the threatening notes and those eerie sounds coming from the attic? Then Sam digs up a hidden tunnel ... but does it lead to treasure or danger?

STRANGE NEIGHBORS

Sam is spellbound by another mystery!

There's a mystery brewing right next door to Sam the sheepdog! Three very odd women have moved in with all sorts of caged animals. Sam is sure her creepy new neighbors are witches. After all, those poor animals look so miserable they must be under a spell. Suddenly Sam isn't feeling well either. Have the witches put a hex on her too? Can Sam, together with Jennie and her best friend Beth, discover the truth before it's too late?